PADDINGTON™

HarperFestival is an imprint of HarperCollins Publishers.

Paddington: Paddington in London
Based on the Paddington novels written and created by Michael Bond
PADDINGTON™ and PADDINGTON BEAR™ © Paddington and Company Limited/
STUDIOCANAL S.A. 2014
For information
address HarperCollins Children's Books, a division of HarperCollins Publishers,
195 Broadway, New York, NY 10007.
www.harpercollinschildrens.com
ISBN 978-0-06-234995-8
    15 16 17 18   CWM   10 9 8 7 6 5 4 3 2
❖
First Edition

PADD🐾INGTON

Paddington in London

Adapted by Annie Auerbach and Mandy Archer

Based on the screenplay written by Paul King

Based on the Paddington Bear novels

written and created by Michael Bond

HARPER FESTIVAL
An Imprint of HarperCollinsPublishers

My adventure began when I traveled from Lima, the capital of Peru, in a giant ship. I hid out of sight for the entire journey. My aunt Lucy sent me off with lots of jars of marmalade so I wouldn't go hungry. After many days, the ship docked in England.

I hid in a mail sack and was unloaded off the ship. I couldn't see where I was going, but I think the mail sack was put onto a train, because I ended up at Paddington Station in London. When I arrived there, I tried to find someone who would give me a home. I had almost given up hope when I met the Browns! Mrs. Brown named me Paddington, after the station.

Paddington is a famous station. I'm proud to share its name.

The Browns took me around London. One of Mr. Brown's favorite places is the Serpentine. It is a lake in the middle of Hyde Park. Mr. Brown comes here to swim. He says that the Serpentine Swimming Club is the oldest swimming club in Britain. They hold a famous race on Christmas Day, and all the swimmers wear only their bathing suits, no matter how cold the water. I don't like the sound of it very much. Since arriving in England, I prefer to stay on dry ground if I can help it.

Mrs. Brown introduced me to Mr. Gruber. He owns an antiques shop full of fascinating things on Portobello Road. It's a street with plenty of hustle and bustle, especially on Saturdays when market traders set up their stalls. I like to visit Mr. Gruber for my elevenses. We share cocoa and buns, and he tells me wonderful stories. He immigrated to England when he was young, just like me.

Something I was fascinated to learn when I arrived in London is that England has a queen. Her Majesty, Queen Elizabeth II, lives in an enormous house. Her home is called Buckingham Palace. Mr. Gruber promised to take me there one day to see the changing of the guard.

When I lived in Peru, I dreamed of coming to London. Aunt Lucy and Uncle Pastuzo had once met an explorer from London, and he taught them about his culture. They, in turn, taught me. But when I arrived and discovered that Big Ben wasn't really a person, but a bell inside a clock tower, I was very surprised. It is still an impressive sight, though! The building itself is called the Elizabeth Tower. (I'm told that not many Londoners even know that!)

There is a place in London called the Geographers' Guild. It's a very famous old society where explorers gather to share their research. I thought it would be a good place to find out about the explorer who knew my aunt and uncle. It's a magnificent center of learning, but I discovered they don't take kindly to strangers. Mr. Brown had to dress in disguise while I hid in his cart.

Another center of learning is the Natural History Museum. This magnificent building is packed to the rafters with fossils, plants, and dinosaur bones.

PERU

PADDINGTON

It also houses an enormous collection of exotic animals that have been stuffed and put on display. Millicent is the director of taxidermy and is responsible for finding new specimens.

The quickest way to travel to all of these places is on the London Underground, but it isn't always easy when you're a bear. I have to be careful I don't get my fur caught in the escalators, and I'm not quite tall enough to reach the ticket barrier.

London is a fascinating place. It's very different from Darkest Peru, but I think I shall enjoy living here.